Gary L. Williams, Esquire is a resident of Laurens, South Carolina. He was conferred a Juris Doctorate degree from the University of South Carolina, Columbia, South Carolina, and has been in the private practice of law for over thirty years.

Dedicated to the writer and art collector, Gertrude Stein.

Gary L. Williams, Esquire

TWO ARMS AND TEN FINGERS

AUSTIN MACAULEY PUBLISHERS®

LONDON · CAMBRIDGE · NEW YORK · SHARJAH

Copyright © Gary L. Williams, Esquire 2025

All rights reserved. No part of this publication may be reproduced, distributed, or transmitted in any form or by any means, including photocopying, recording, or other electronic or mechanical methods, without the prior written permission of the publisher, except in the case of brief quotations embodied in critical reviews and certain other non-commercial uses permitted by copyright law. For permission requests, write to the publisher.

Any person who commits any unauthorized act in relation to this publication may be liable to criminal prosecution and civil claims for damages.

This is a work of fiction. Names, characters, businesses, places, events, locales, and incidents are either the products of the author's imagination or used in a fictitious manner. Any resemblance to actual persons, living or dead, or actual events is purely coincidental.

Ordering Information
Quantity sales: Special discounts are available on quantity purchases by corporations, associations, and others. For details, contact the publisher at the address below.

Publisher's Cataloging-in-Publication data
Williams, Esquire, Gary L.
Two Arms and Ten Fingers

ISBN 9798895432266 (Paperback)
ISBN 9798895432273 (Hardback)
ISBN 9798895432297 (ePub e-book)
ISBN 9798895432280 (Audiobook)

Library of Congress Control Number: 2024926538

www.austinmacauley.com/us

First Published 2025
Austin Macauley Publishers LLC
40 Wall Street, 33rd Floor, Suite 3302
New York, NY 10005
USA

mail-usa@austinmacauley.com
+1 (646) 5125767

I acknowledge those who are forgiven and those who must be forgiven.

Prologue

For there is nothing hidden except to be made visible; nothing is secret except to come to the light…

The Gospel of Mark, Chapter 4, Verse 22

1

In the small and quaint town of Milton, Massachusetts, two arms and ten fingers gently awaken as they freely swept into the cool winter breeze. An unusually lazy Saturday afternoon found a panic-stricken doctor, Nancy Kilburn, sipping the bottom half of her warm morning coffee as she exercised the stiffness from her aging arms and fingers. The 35-year-old obstetrician became mesmerized by the majestic beauty of the snow-covered woods outside her home's large beveled window while asking the poet, John Keats, to deliver his 19-century prose and giving the words that her enchanted eyes perceived. Only, the great Keats could stir the necessary stanzas as required similar to the first words of the first hymn at any early evening's vespers service.

"A thing of beauty is a joy forever;
Its loveliness increase; it will never
Pass into nothingness; but still will keep
A bower quiet for us, and a sleep
Full of sweet dreams, and health, and quiet breathing,
Therefore, on every morrow, are we wreathing
A flowery band to bind us to the earth,

Spite of despondence, of the inhuman dearth
Of noble natures, of the gloomy days;
Of all the unhealthy and o'er-darkened ways
Made for our searching; yes, in spite of all,
Some shape of beauty moves away the pall......"

As the last words resounded in Nancy's memory, this incredible view of earth's glory broaden into another day's journey which helped gently calm her worried spirit. Her life's focus had always been on her medical career with no time to seriously think of family, friends, having children of her own or managing her finances. The only real humans in her world where the small ones, the very small babies that were delivered with her skilled two arms and ten fingers while crying and holding out their own two arms and ten fingers. She looked upon the wondrous woods and her own poetic words came upon her spirit.

"Two arms have I
To lift and caress
To help adorable babies breathe
Their first breaths of life.

I hear their cries,
Their mother's voice,
Yet, I see my
Ten fingers as safety nets
For life.
Out of the holy womb,
Another soul begins its
Journey,

To see what shall be seen, heard,
And touched."

Yes, Dr. Kilburn cradled the precious ones as they opened their small and searching eyes to announce God's continued presence, an awakening of pure innocence of God's infinite holiness. Small, soft round circles of beauty seemed to suddenly appear from a heavenly realm as each mother felt relief of their baby's delivery and Dr. Kilburn found herself staring into that unimaginable beauty as the babies cried, not wanting to be taken from such a peaceful place. Often Dr. Kilburn would ponder whether their personalities formed primarily from their mother's own thoughts or had each baby received heavenly assignments.

She thought fondly of a mother who had believed that her child while yet in the womb had been marked by a large black snake slithering along the mother's front porch as it wrapped its huge sleek body around an old wooden post. The mother eagerly awaited an answer as to whether her child would be born with snake-like features, and so intently was the mother's inspection as to the child's features and movements she became very much disturbed when the child had appeared with interesting green eyes and began shaking primarily due to epilepsy. Unfortunately, the mother believed that it was due to the snake. Baby after precious baby flashed into Dr. Kilburn's mind as the warmth of her morning coffee and the coolness of the winter breeze blew casually through the walnut trees as she watched each snowflake slowly fall into its perfect space.

As John Keats' poem continued to resonate, Dr. Kilburn's own personal life ascended on her life's grand virtual stage appearing as if it were Shakespeare's Globe theater's stage on the banks of the meandering river, Thames in London. A single giant walnut tree came forth to her view entwining the memories of delivering hundreds, if not thousands of babies.

"What could her future be other than to be a doctor and seeing their little arms and fingers reaching into the small world of Milton?" she concluded. "No other profession could have provided this level of satisfaction."

Now, her hands and fingers constantly smelled of childbirth and from time to time ached due to years of paternity labor. Thankfully, she was born with large and broad shoulders which helped those arms, hands, and fingers skillfully deliver each baby. Her life's veil continued to pronounce and she saw herself as a child, happy without a care while hearing her own mother's voice.

"Nancy, my love, you're my baby and the world is waiting on you to do great things." Now, she looked into the falling snow and late afternoon sun. Her mother's sweet voice became as clear as if her words were spoken just seconds ago while she was happily cuddled in her dear mother's two arms and ten fingers. Her mother's voice continued to speak in a long-ago poem that her mother would often say as she awaken:

"Springtime…we stretch
All two arms and ten fingers
High in the sky
For ten fingers match
Our ten toes
That we may stand and play

And tell God thank you for
This fresh new season of time."

Memories of her 16th birthday were followed by joyful college days and her honorable medical school graduation; and suddenly, her very first patient appeared, a premature baby weighing only four pounds, but full of life. Humbly, the parents were so thankful that her medical skills helped save her life. Nancy remembered how life was beautiful as day by day, moment by moment she used the medical knowledge to foster life while the parents desperately prayed and hoped for miracles as each baby in her memory magically came forth. Names such as Sydney, Royce, and Jefferson all crying and screaming with their two arms and ten fingers flailing into the air, yearning for life.

She continued to sip the last of her warm coffee and gradually, as if in the days of the biblical Noah, a virtual storm cloud descended upon her happy memories. The beauty of the woods outside her beveled window seemed to become a pall that covered her memories just as the poet, Yeats announced in his poem. The ominous clouds began to hover directly over her long comfortable couch as she was summoned to remember her frantic financial condition that made her tears flowed, eye buckets of tears, full of water and age. She cried for the torment stress of her student loans and monthly budget, begging for a solution. Suddenly her memories were interrupted by a telephone call.

"Hello," a familiar voice sounded. "Dr. Kilburn, Dr. Kilburn, you are needed in the delivery room."

Gallantly and without awaiting further recollection of her past, she happily went to her Milton Memorial

Hospital's paternity department responsibly, forgetting her financial worries and focusing on her medical duties as another small life was about to come into the world. Dr. Kilburn once again became the happy obstetrician that she had always been.

It was late in the night when Dr. Kilburn returned from another successful delivery and her young legs felt tired, seemingly, two lazy spectators that watched as her other body parts decidedly were uncooperative for rest. She again felt a warmth in her spirit and the gentle voice of her mother wisely beckoned her in memory.

"Nancy, get your lessons. Study so as to think not just to memorialize, whatever you encounter in life, you can calmly find the answers." Hearing her mother's advice fortified her resolve that on Monday, she would drive to Westbury, a town 30 miles away to find a better quality of life she so desperately needed.

Thus, began one of the best doctors of Massachusetts journey out of the small and quaint New England town of Milton as she confidently applied to both hospitals of the nearby town of Westbury. Relatively, new hospitals, Amherst Memorial Hospital and Foster General Hospital could provide a higher income, and as she walked to the front door of Amherst Memorial, she so happened to see a doctor who she had known since medical school, Dr. Artemus Archell. He walked briskly with his two arms and ten fingers swinging in his long white doctor's coat, an excellent surgeon who had been practicing medicine for over 40 years and a much-respected member of the medical profession.

Dr. Archell excitedly said, "Hi, Nancy, how's it going? I haven't seen you since our days at Staton Medical. It's been a couple of years."

She gladly retorted, "Well, it's going. I'm looking for a new start, a new position."

Almost overlapping her voice, Dr. Archell exclaimed, "Well, I'm happy to see you. Amherst Memorial has been good to me. I've been here so long. Seems like I even helped to lay each limestone block." They both chuckled as he said with perplexity, "But I thought you were satisfied in Milton."

Dr. Kilburn, with her brown eyes of distress, said, "Well, no, financially the small town cannot currently support my cavalier lifestyle." Laughingly, she added, "Don't get me wrong; I love Milton, but I had all these student loans and, being single, I need either a higher income, a bankruptcy lawyer or a 'sugar daddy'."

As they laughed, Dr. Archell said, "Well, I'll help you find a position here. It's a progressive hospital because they purchase the latest technology and the hospital's administration listens with a truly state of the art paternity ward that delivers the highest number of babies in the state. You would be an excellent choice to head that department and you know, Nancy, I guess with all these baby deliveries, this community is doing more than just reading books."

As they laughed, Dr. Archell again exclaimed his sincere happiness of seeing her again and, true to his word, he gave a great recommendation. Thereafter, life for Dr. Nancy Kilburn moved majestically forward; that is, Dr. Nancy Kilburn of Milton became Dr. Nancy Kilburn, chief obstetrician, Amherst Memorial Hospital, Westbury, Massachusetts.

2

A few miles from Dr. Kilburn's new Westbury home found a worried mortician, Mr. Edgar Fielding sitting in his small dusty office. Born in Westbury, he had no fresh dead bodies to transport and his stressful eyes stared into that darkened emptiness, and emphatically he screamed into the darkness, "How must I handle these bills? Every month I'm short, every month! Oh, Dad, how I need you now! How could you die and leave me?" His dad's two arms and ten fingers had carefully gripped many an expensive casket, producing a successful and vibrant funeral home business. Now, his son's two arms and ten fingers were holding a large monthly utility bill that needed to be immediately paid while his business had begun to dramatically constrict and a drastically reduction in income and now as an older man of 55, he had to make some important financial decisions.

Years of handling funeral matters, his hands and fingers smelled of formaldehyde and death with his social interaction centered principally on helping sincere, fragile, and grieving families. Now weeks would now pass without a call for his funeral services that made him understandably concerned for gone were the days of four to six families per week making arrangements. Yet, not due to the excellent quality of Fielding funeral home services, but for Westbury's surrounding areas lifespans having improved since the community's doctors were saving many more lives. The misty veil of his last funeral appeared to his worried conscious; a horrid affair where a 35-year-old had been violently decapitated, a straight cut to a round neck and his loving family demanded that his body be life-like when presented to the family. Yet, initially the body was far from being recognizable since the deceased's head was found in a concrete vat. Tirelessly, Mr. Fielding had worked into the late hours of night bringing back the man as if an Egyptian sarcophagus had been opened, a mummy exposed, and body parts reattached.

Memories flooded into shadows as Mr. Fielding attempted to justify why he never had gone into another profession. Sadly, he recalled a poem he had made when he was just a young mortician surrounded with an oversupply of dead bodies.

"I have but two arms
And ten fingers
Carrying them to the grave;

A grave that had been awaiting
Them since birth.

I have but two arms and
Ten fingers to present them well
As they lay confined in space,
Carried by five and me,
As the boxes covered by the pall
Roll into their grave."

Yes, the great poet Keats would cast a queer eye as to whether Mr. Fielding had been memorizing one of his stanzas. When Mr. Fielding was a 12-year-old child, his father, Edward had taken him to Westbury's Sullivan funeral parlor. This historic parlor since the 1800s was where the real work of embalming and preparation of bodies was then done in Westbury. A small brightly lit room where the dead bodies were taken from long black hearses only to be laid on long white tables as each body stretched out in their long sleep; yet, waiting for the after-life. Each of the embalmer's two arms and ten fingers gently worked as they made the precise cuts removing and draining the old red liquid that had turned blue into a large blood-filled tank to be replaced with embalming fluid. All of this morbid process stayed vividly in the young Fielding's mind throughout his teenage years and into adulthood resulting in his definitive career choice.

The Fielding's funeral home had begun in 1932, a stable business through the preceding years. All the town's morticians were suffering for there were three mortuaries; Fielding's, Sullivan's, and Hunter's funeral home and now just too many funeral homes for the small population of ten thousand. The competition for the small amount of bodies escalated into a tale of three large and hungry buzzards. The Fielding funeral home's financial situation became a weekly, if not, daily issue as profit margins began to plummet while utilities and other bills increased and this bill, yes, this utility bill handled so gently within his large clubby fingers weighted the heaviest upon his mind.

A nice man who provided a wonderful caring funeral service; financial mismanagement of his funeral business was his tragedy. Now, if only he would file the necessary bankruptcy paperwork, he just might obtain the financial relief needed to continue to exist. As his two arms and ten fingers slowly handled and observed this utility bill, his eyes began to tear, big tears. With his big tears on this particular Saturday, a very Last Will and Testament also lay on his big oak desk next to a large and waiting 38-caliber handgun. A solid black mussel with a white and brownish handle and a well-oiled trigger allowing the slightest pressure to release its bullet and solve any problem. He knew that unless someone died right away requesting his funeral service, there would be no more cash to pay this bill or any other bill so he thought that his 55-year-old remains; maybe, his dead body was needed for this business to continue and pay its bills. Out of the darkness, his dad's voice came as a clarion call of attempted salvation.

Firmly, the voice spoke, "Son, there shall be cycles, business cycles, and you must save in the good times."

In his lonely funeral parlor, he began to feel at the very least he had let his father down and a nervous breakdown was required. As his tears came within his water-soaked eyes and upon his rosy cheeks, the mist from his eyes floated in the air fogging his spectacles as he sat with his body folded like a much-played accordion needing a rhapsody. At his desk, he casually handled his huge bill with his long, straight nose sitting well centered upon it. As he stretched, entertaining his nose were two brown eyes, his Last Will and Testament, and a possible bullet from his handgun while Gershwin's Rhapsody in Blue seemed to begin to play in the dusty funeral parlor office's air. He began to recall his days when he was young, vibrant, and prosperous, as those four to six bodies would arrive each week for him to apply his craft. At that time, his mortuary was one of the busiest and best and as he remembered the little kids with only one parent, as the other lay in his parlor as he tried to console:

"You see these five fingers
I got five more
(As his other hand appeared from its hiding place behind his back)
Ten fingers attached
To these two arms
Isn't that so;
(while the children nodded in their agreement)

You should know
I use the two to
Carry the ten
I can do wonderful
And marvelous things
With these ten fingers
Carried by these two arms
Yet, two arms and ten fingers
I have only one brain."

As the children laughed, their minds became refocused somewhat so that he could talk money with their remaining parent.

In the misty veil of life, there appeared his wonderful parents as he became the funeral business director for the very first time; and the joy and happy memories surrounding his accomplishment with that grand opening. Also, in his life's misty corridors, suddenly, there appeared his parlor's first dead body, a 13-year-old child whose life was shorten after a tragic bicycle accident. A teenage girl who had just received her driver's permit veered into the child bicycle's path. Strangely, as Gershwin's rhapsody began to play the lower piano keys, there was also his first funeral service as he calmly walked down the center church aisle to close his very first coffin. Yes, this morbid scene was Mr. Fielding's beginnings while prosperity had followed, but that was until the funds that he had grown accustomed began to fluctuate in a downward spiral. Suddenly, there appeared the present reality where the shameful veil was lifted on his financial probabilities while the three possible answers laid on his desk and one answer in particular.

The moments began to drift into hours. He quietly continued to reminisce while the last notes of Gershwin's rhapsody had long dissipated into the parlor's dusty air. Suddenly, his funeral home's telephone rang. Startled, as if he had seen a coffin's lid open at his own graveside service;

Mr. Fielding answered in his usual caring voice, "Fielding's funeral home, how may we help you?"

A familiar voice said, "This is Amherst Memorial. We sadly have a deceased baby in our hospital's morgue. The family has requested Fielding."

As he stumbled over his now-static and vivid memories, he somehow composed himself, releasing calming words from his very stiff parched lips, "Yes, I'm on my way."

He placed the urgent utility bill once again on his desk next to his Last Will and Testament along with his 38 handgun. He breathed an ecstatic sigh of relief for he thought that just maybe, he could turn this unusual fateful telephone call into the necessary funds needed so that his middle-aged body would not be a necessary business customer. His two arms and ten fingers fumbled in the dusty and darken office for his hearse's keys and a strange, uninhibited smile came to his placid face as his own fragile life focused not on his death, but on the death awaiting him at the hospital.

The deceased child was a six-year-old child who had been killed innocently playing with his father's handgun. As Mr. Fielding looked upon this departed soul, he remembered how only a couple of moments ago he had intently considered giving himself a bullet. As he placed the young child in his transport coffin, a cold chill came upon him as he observed the child's chest appearing like a hollow inside a cave. Although he had done this meet-and-greet process hundreds of time, if not thousands, he placed the small body in his hearse and began to cry. He thought:

I am a man
Who needs a plan
Some might say

It could be discovered
Over a cup of tea
I say,
If one really queries
It would be so easy to see.

So I pondered many a night
To find enough
Coffin lids to close tight;
So that I and the dead
Shall have peace
For eternity.

While driving to his small embalming room, Mr. Edgar Fielding of Westbury, Massachusetts, thought of how the parents would miss their wonderful son; more importantly, he thought how his utility bill would now be paid. This pleasant thought caused the edges of his mouth to again curl around the long point of his nose which was centered in the middle of his very rosy cheeks.

3

Yes, Westbury, Massachusetts, became home for both Dr. Nancy Kilburn at Amherst Memorial Hospital and Mr. Edgar Fielding of the Fielding's funeral home. Two honest hard-working professionals whose financial problems led them to plea for a savior with life-changing solutions. Dr. Kilburn's new apartment was conveniently next door to the hospital and adjacent to a very large, well-kept Westbury Heights cemetery where hundreds of large distinguished tombstones spread over several acres proclaiming the epitaphs of Westbury's best citizens. The well-manicured cemetery provided a back-drop to a brilliantly green space known as Magnolia Community Park.

Several months later, Dr. Kilburn finally began to relax and each Sunday was her day, a much-needed rest day where she found joy in visiting the park and unwinding while easing her mind from the daily routine of delivering babies. She would lay beneath her usual oak tree and on her usual bright orange blanket given to her by her mother, Maybelle. Each Sunday, children would be joyfully playing and enjoying themselves. Mothers would be strolling their precious babies and, from time to time, people would stop and chat, showing respect and telling of their baby's progress.

Fate came to Dr. Kilburn while at Magnolia Community Park, for one beautiful Sunday, Dr. Kilburn was enjoying the best-selling book, *A Soldier Dies to Live* beneath the big oak when a large red ball rolled over and met at her blanket's edge. This ball with red rose flowers imprinted on each side seemed to be two rolling flowers looking for a well-cultivated garden. As she turned her head to investigate, she heard a voice, "I think those two small girls over there are responsible for your sunny interruption."

Looking in the direction of the unfamiliar voice, she saw a man, an older man who seemed welcoming and inclined on a park bench.

"Hey, I'm Edgar, Mr. Edgar Fielding. I was sitting here watching you just enjoying and reading your book when I saw the ball. I see that you were reading the author, Esquire Williams."

"Yes, Gary!"

"Hi, I'm Dr. Nancy Kilburn. Yes, I've enjoyed his book so far; it's about a man who shoots himself and as he slowly dies, he realizes that life is more vibrant than he would ever know. It's so intriguing because this large colorful parrot helps him explore life's wonder."

Mr. Fielding's mind became entranced with less upon her words and more on Nancy's beauty when he realized that her wavering lips were not moving. He excitedly said, "I read Williams' book, *'Revolutionary Voices from the Slave Houses'* and found it indeed good reading from the perspective of the enslaved. You know, everyone talks about patriots, battlefields, and roses when it comes to the

American Revolution; but what were the enslaved's thoughts of freedom? Seems to me, the American patriots thought of themselves and not true freedom for all."

As Mr. Fielding continued to try to share Dr. Kilburn's space and especially the one between her ears, he added, "You are a beautiful spirit, glad to meet you."

As Dr. Kilburn gathered herself, she politely said, "I come here every Sunday. Maybe, I'll see you next Sunday."

"You know, I should have warned you about the incoming giant ball; but it was too late. I was trying to write my latest poem entitled: *And She Will Awaken*. May I read you some of it? You know, one of my passions since I was a small boy is poetry."

Exuberantly, Dr. Kilburn said, "Yes, I love poetry." As Mr. Fielding adjusted his starched collar, an uneasy silence came between them as the children's voices could be heard joyfully playing. Mr. Fielding looked into a misty trance-like veil, cleared his throat, and began:

"Yes, she will awaken,
One bright morning for
She only sleeps;
She shall awaken;
In a land so calm and true.

When that time comes
Joy shall be known,
Wonderful life shall be renewed.

Yes, there is a river
That runs for eternal time,
Which began when
The universe was anew.

She shall awaken
To find joy,
Trouble shall be no more
Yes, life is a river, eternal

She only sleeps,
For she shall awaken
A few more winters
That shall turn to spring,
Life shall only
Begin again,
We all shall be there in the melodies
Of the summer with her again
For she shall awaken."

As Mr. Fielding's voice raised with each word, Nancy Kilburn felt the sincerity of his words, as she said, "That was nice and thoughtful. We both love words to help us relax, you with your poetry and me with my books and I was enjoying my quiet time when this ball came wandering into my meditation space."

They shared a laugh and as Nancy continued to tell him how she enjoyed the poem. The two girls that had been near the middle of the park came running over;

"Sorry," they said, as if they were in a choir, as the doctor retorted, "Here you go!"

Fielding continued. "Well, you know I'm in the funeral home business waiting for the phone to ring, so I have quite a lot of time to write poetry."

Nancy said, "I deal with the beginning of life and you with the ending."

As Mr. Fielding said, "Let me share with you another poem. Well, I had this family whose mother had died and they sat around the chapel crying and every now and then one of the family members would go up to the casket and look, and I watched them as I stood."

Jordan River shall always be
For life is like a river;
Flowing; and
With every drop
You will not step into the same
Part twice;
Life continues;
Human beings are much like this river,
Flowing into eternity.

Joyfully, after the giant ball incident and various poems, Sunday after Sunday, Dr. Kilburn and Mr. Fielding shared their ups and downs of their weekly lives, she telling him of delivering babies and him sharing his latest poems and telling her of the current community or lack thereof of deaths. Always, he would sort his business inventory to her in morbid detail, telling of the many bodies taken to the nearby Westbury Heights cemetery and beyond. These type of conversations are how their friendly relationship began as they both enjoyed the park, flowers, books, poetry and sharing their lives.

Unbeknownst to them, this first meeting would lead only a few months later to Dr. Nancy Kilburn becoming Dr. Nancy Kilburn-Fielding. Each Sunday, 'Fielding', as she affectionately began calling him, would have poems for her; and one particular Sunday, Fielding gave himself the courage to say, "I have a special poem for you today," and with trembling fingers that seemed more like noodles boiling in hot water, he began:

"Please, Nancy give me back my heart;
Nancy Kilburn, I love you
My life has been one of cold late night hearse rides;
I searched for a flower among all the flowers
Of a garden;
I strolled through lonely times
Shapeless valentines;
I alone saw the beauty of a sunset, the mountains,
The ocean;

Well, you came into my life
When life was a hollowness
Of isolation and worry.

You made me want to live again,
To share again,
To just be again

Yes, my life shall now be complete,
If you allow me to place,
This diamond ring on your finger."

As he bent his two arms and ten fingers, Mr. Edgar Fielding placed a two-carat diamond ring on Dr. Nancy Kilburn's left finger; and while holding her two arms and ten fingers into his, Fielding ended his poem by saying, "Please be my wife. Yes, you indeed are my flower among all the flowers."

Nancy, startled as her soft brown eyes gently flickered, began, "Oh, Fielding, I feel the same. Yes, I will marry you. You have come into my life when my world was work, career, and more work. We have shared many a laugh beneath this old oak. I also am ready to take the next step. Oh, I shall love you forever. You are the one who has come upon my island of despair, loneliness, and heartache so that I could be rescued. Yes, yes, I will marry you!"

4

114 Elm Street, Westbury, Massachusetts, a small house on a small hill near a small stream became Edgar and Nancy Fielding's home. The Fielding's love of flowers and walnut trees was evident and most days, especially the sunny ones, neighbors would be joyfully playing with their kids while tending to their immaculate lawns. Families such as the Emersons, Cartwrights, Abercrombies, and Kellets, all were professionals with busy schedules who valued their privacy.

One family in particular, the Lawsons, Mr. And Mrs. Tom and Allie Lawson seemed to become Fieldings' best friends as they enjoyed weekly dinners. Tom was like a man who began as an explorer, an adventurer in life only to get in a cyclonic wilderness of age and despair, yet, if ever he would find his way again to his main life's pathway; he could finally begin again. His wife, Allie was very much a quiet, reserved and careful person. A housewife that most times found Tom beginning and being the topic of conversation as Allie quietly sat by his side like a French poodle waiting its owner's direction. Most dinners as she sat, a poem would resoundingly repeat within her spirit to her conscience so that she could get through Tom's long run-on conversations:

"Quietly, I sat
Carefully eating a meal
Using my two arms
And ten fingers

I listen but do not speak
Just until,
My brain freezes as I
Hear the lies,

I am not happy,
But who cares but me
My introductory
Sentence ends with I am Allie.
Yes, Allie who came from the north looking for honesty,
And genius;

I found deceit.
Now I sat awaiting my
Chance to leave."

It was if the great poet and thinker Gertude Stein had awaken in Allie from her New York pedestal behind Manhattan's main library as she guarded the large marble lions, especially when Ms. Stein announced:

"One must dare to be happy. It takes a lot of time to be a genius. You have to sit around so much, doing nothing, really doing nothing. Everybody knows if you are too careful, you are so occupied in being careful that you are sure to stumble over something."

Such was Allies' life and with more visits and dinners, Tom, a lawyer seem to be less intrigued with the wine, dinners, and conversation and more with Nancy. Each time he would arrive for dinner, it seemed that his hazel eyes led to Nancy's creative soul. The only other thing Tom enjoyed more, that is, other than romancing other people's wives and Mr. Fielding's wife in particular, was talking about his lawn for every Saturday morning beginning exactly at ten; not ten of ten and not ten after ten but precisely ten o'clock; Tom would mow and care for his lawn such as Stradivarius with his violins or Mozart with his musical notes, always repeating his favorite saying, "I love perfection, perfection, perfection." His lawn was one of extreme organization with beautiful red roses. A long and desirable walkway extending down the lawn's center appeared like it was a red carpet missing a center. As months went by, Tom's lawn-mowing skills began to regularly benefit not only his own lawn; but the Fielding's address for his focus became Dr. Nancy Kilburn-Fielding. An experienced lawyer, Thomas Lawson Esquire, better known as Tom, had been practicing 30 years but had grown tired of clients and their concerns. He felt like a dumping ground for his clients' problems with one in particular, leading him to realize that he should find another way of earning a living. The client, a Mr. Cosbury Eagleton had become so violent toward his wife that he was charged with criminal domestic violence. Tom's legal skills produced a dismissal; but tragically, as soon as the dismissal was filed, Mr. Eagleton killed his 'beloved' wife. Thereafter, Tom's office door began to stay closed with only an occasional cleaning of the door's cobwebs and his life would be encapsulated into a drink called Negroni. Yes, bitter, vermouth, gin with only a small slice of lemon, his regular mixed drink that was a substitute for oxygen.

Tom's weekdays began with Negronis and ended with Negronis but also with thoughts of Nancy. She added life to his once-dying corpse. A 63-year-old corpse that could have been lying in Nancy's husband's small embalming room and on display years ago. His marriage to Allie who he had met in her hometown of Nova Scotia, Canada, had grown old and dull and it was as if Tom Lawson were waiting on a long, dark train that slowly moved into darkened tunnels of infinity. Sometimes in his drunken stupor, he would shout:

"With these two arms
And ten fingers
I used to swing courthouse doors
Looking for justice to appear;
I looked for the
Blind-folded lady
But sometimes
She just lifted her veil.

I shouted,
Where is the justice
When some are treated
Differ
And the lady with a stern look in her eye
Said,
"I may have a large floppy blind-fold upon my eyes;
But my ears hear well.
I listen for the codes,

The codes of wealth and power;
For as the facts are announced
I, justice rule as I please."

He once was the romantic that Allie desired. Now he was a man who only sought his own personal pleasure. Months passed and Tom and Nancy's relationship grew as Fielding and Allie became only sounding boards much like excess baggage. Just as Nancy and Fielding love of poetry began their relationship, he and Nancy's love for the same poetry and her vibrant love of life drew his interest to where their dinners along with his regularly caring for her lawn led to romance. As Fielding focused on his morbid cyclical funeral trade, each week, Tom would cut his lawn and see Fielding's return to his funeral parlor quietly saying to himself as Fielding got in his car and drove away, while Tom said, "Perfection, Perfection, Perfection."

5

In 1968, the Fieldings welcomed a sweet baby girl named Heather, and once again the financial storms gathered because of the higher expense of three. In retrospect, two financial imbeciles should not have married. They brought their financial abilities or rather lack, thereof dooming their happiness. Nancy knew that the real truth was that Edgar Fielding was not the father and as their combined financial bills mounted, the Fieldings faced the stress of it all, which accompanied long and dreadful stares into darkness. It seemed bankruptcy became their only option as Heather grew and Nancy became more concerned that the baby looked more like Tom than Fielding. Nancy hurriedly approached Fielding with the idea of adoption.

"Fielding, here we are lacking money. I think adoption would allow us a new start." Heather would be better off with someone more financially stable! Thus, little Heather was placed for adoption through Tom's legal skills; and unfortunately, financial concerns continued to mount which led Fielding to confide in his friend, Tom. Unbeknownst to Fielding, Tom had already known about their financial troubles while Nancy had laid in his two arms with his rather long ten fingers slowly caressing her long blond and shoulder-length hair. Night after night, Fielding tried to come up with a viable plan and, week after week, Tom enjoyed his wife. One Saturday night, after their weekly dinner, Tom and Fielding shared an after-dinner cigar on the porch; and later Fielding said, "Nancy, Tom has given me, I think, an interesting and creative plan and is one that if we were ever discovered we would be jailed for quite a long time."

As Fielding explained the details, Nancy intensely said, "No! No! No! We would lose all we have ever worked for in life, absolutely not." Days passed and Nancy looked into Fielding's soft brown and worried eyes, remembering why she had little Heather adopted.

Nancy unexpectedly said, "Look at these bills. If we don't do something, we will be living on the streets. Tell me again of this plan."

And as she listened, Fielding slowly presented the details, "Well, since you are an outstanding obstetrician who deliver babies at Amherst Hospital, you should tell some of the mothers and fathers that their precious babies were still-born and after such sad notification to the parents, direct the hospital to call me. I will transport the babies alive from the hospital in my funeral hearse and protect them in a specially made coffin with air holes cut in the coffin-lid's top for breathing. Our friend, neighbor, and lawyer, Tom will use his legal skills and place each baby for adoption and each baby's adoption would earn us 100,000 dollars. The plan would save us financially and no one will be the wiser."

As Nancy listened, the edges of her mouth curled upward and sharply pointed to her big nose centered squarely between her two red and rosy cheeks. Dr. Nancy Kilburn-Fielding, while knowing that her medical license and freedom were jeopardized, decided that this ingenious plan was well worth a try so that she and Tom could continue to live in their wonderful world of deception.

6

One evening, as the Fieldings and the Lawsons shared a dinner, Fielding and Tom sat once again on the Fielding's front porch.

"You know, Tom, this plan is great. Well, Tom," Nancy said, "yes and we all know the plan. But carefully implementation is another story. You do your part and we will do ours, and within three to four years, I will retire and think about palm trees, round hips and Margaritas." As both sipped their Negronis, Fielding added, "Yes, Nancy believes that it might just work."

Tom exclaimed, "Great, I believe all of us will be pleased. Your Margaritas are already made and waiting on you in two to three years because I have 20 clients who are desperately wanting babies and willing to pay. Yes, that's one million for you and one for you and Nancy."

As they laughed, a summer storm approached blowing rain and wind and taking their creative idea of greed and illegality quickly into the house.

The next week, the first baby became the first adopted baby of their scheme, and thereafter, baby after baby was delivered by Dr. Kilburn-Fielding's two arms and ten fingers. Healthy and rosy, the babies came crying into the newness of life. Yet, Dr. Kilburn whose heart had turned to deceit and greed manipulated the system and wholeheartedly signed death certificates for their transport. Indeed, Fielding's funeral home was called and the middle man, Edgar Fielding, carefully and with his two arms and ten fingers methodically placed each child in the long, black hearse as he drove to meet the lawyer, Tom. Each baby delivered with two arms and ten fingers and each baby with their two arms and ten fingers began life; but unfortunately, instead of cuddling into their mother's arms, they began a ride to Tom's law office, and Tom, with his two arms and ten fingers, created 'legal' documents to smoothly complete the adoption. Each time, as he drove, Fielding often wondered,

Who would adopt and how would the adoptive parents show their love? What would this child become in life? Would one of them become a mortician? A doctor? Or a lawyer?

One cloudy day, as Mr. Fielding was transporting the next baby, a city of Westbury police officer suddenly flashed his blue lights, stopping Fielding. As the officer walked to the driver's side of Fielding's hearse, he asked Mr. Fielding for his license and registration. Angrily, the officer said, "Do you realize you were speeding?"

Fielding said, "No. Officer", I was so much concentrating on getting this dead child to my funeral home just right down the street. The officer had known Fielding for as long as he had known himself, and as the officer looked at Fielding's license, he said, "Well, Mr. Edgar, this time, I will give you a traffic warning, but you must slow down."

Exhaling a sigh of relief, Fielding gladly said, "Thank you." But as the officer slowly turned, a loud and unmistakably baby's cry was heard.

"What was that? Sounded like a baby?"

Fielding said, "What was what?"

As the officer began to look in the hearse's back compartment, the baby's cries became louder and the officer realized that the cry was coming from the small coffin.

"Mr. Fielding, I think there's a live baby in this coffin back here!"

As Mr. Fielding heard, he clearly said, "I know not!" However, as the small white coffin was slowly slid out with the officer's two arms and ten fingers, the coffin was opened and there appeared a tiny and very rosy baby begging for life with its own flailing two arms and ten fingers.

Fielding was arrested and charged with kidnapping. The baby's mother, Ms. Roxy Davis, was informed and at the bond hearing, Mrs. Davis' two arms and ten fingers stretched to the courthouse's historic ceiling while she fainted and blamed Mr. Fielding for handling her baby as just another cemetery package. The judge considered the possibility of more missing children and denied bond, and a jury trial date was announced. Fielding knew that his wife, Nancy's, and Tom's lives depended on his testimony. If he told of their intricate adoption plan, all of them would be in jeopardy, and with his love for Nancy and respect for Tom, Fielding kept his mouth closed as he reasoned, "If declared guilty by the jury, I shall accept all of the penalty."

In a red spiral notebook, he wrote a poem:

"Jury trials are new to this old worn man,
Twelve citizens of Westbury
Determining the mortician's fate;

A story that
Shall be polished and
Presented to them.
As I sit, I see my characters appear;
Awaiting the final curtain Shakespeare
Shall whisper,
Comedy or indeed tragedy."

The potential jurors came into the old courtroom. Fielding saw many a family member that had required his funeral services and Nancy saw many a mother who had depended on her to birth their baby. Tom had found a good criminal lawyer, her name, Emily Cano. Ms. Cano seemed to be a brain covered in gray hair, a criminal defense lawyer who had won many of his jury trials, especially the ones that involved murder. Fielding was impressed to find that Cano had just won the trial of a woman who had shot her boyfriend in the back after pleading self-defense. The case centered upon the lady whose boyfriend had turned his back towards her only in an attempt to come around with his fist for a deadly blow when he was shot. Cano had successfully argued self-defense.

Fielding said, "You know, with no confession, the state had only a circumstantial case at best."

The police noted that your wife had signed many a death certificate and in particular, the one for Mrs. Davis' baby.

"Yet, since she was married to you, she could not be made to testify. The City, thus, has to prove their case beyond a reasonable doubt to 12 impartial jurors of Westbury with no direct evidence."

As the jury was selected, Fielding stressfully stared into Nancy's eyes, he saw the saddened mother of little Heather who had been adopted. Yet, he relaxed as if Billie Holiday had begun to sing about 'stormy weather'. He knew if guilty, Nancy would be financially able to survive without him. Judgment day had come, as the 12 jurors were placed in the jury box, Fielding, Nancy, and Tom stared into each other's dark eyes knowing their lives could very well be completely exposed. The state's opening argument, the prosecutor loudly announced, "That a bad guy was present in the courtroom, one who kidnaps little babies and continued by detailing how Edgar Fielding had been stopped, speeding, in the City of Westbury on Jackson Street and a small white coffin that Mr. Fielding had taken from Amherst Hospital and there within that coffin was a live baby."

Ms. Cano made an impassioned opening statement reflecting that Edgar Fielding had no idea the baby in which he was transporting was alive and that it was all an honest mistake at the hospital, an unfortunate accident. Mr. Fielding had no intent to kidnap or take any baby and that the hospital had authorized him to receive the young deceased baby's body and so he did.

Cano stood confidently and articulated, "The United States Constitution is the supreme law of our land. Mr.

Fielding sits in this courtroom presumed innocent unless and until it is proven, this allegation of kidnapping beyond a reasonable doubt. A reasonable doubt is what makes a reasonable person such as yourselves hesitate. Yes, it's like you telling yourself, wait a minute, it's something wrong here."

Then, Ms. Cano said a phrase that resonated throughout the quietness of the courtroom.

She said, "This case is like a rotten apple in the mouth of a skunk. The more you dig into the old rotten apple, the more it smells."

Each juror looked as if they knew aliens were real while the judge curiously looked from the top of his eyeglasses with his rosy cheeks as Cano continued, "Mr. Fielding does not have to testify and the United States Constitution states that you the jury cannot hold this against him."

As Ms. Cano ended his statement, she once again sat beside Fielding. The officer and the administrator of the hospital were called by the District Attorney and each gave their testimony; but surprisingly, the prosecution rested after only two witnesses and as the judge questioned Fielding, Fielding decided not to testify.

The jury received the case and the jury was only out of the courtroom 30 minutes as the foreman gave the jury's answer to the judge. All were quiet. Suddenly, the silence was only broken when the Clerk of Court, Mrs. Rachel Simmons began reading, "The City vs. Edgar Fielding, we the jury, find the defendant, Edgar Fielding, not guilty."

Suddenly, Fielding jumped to his feet, crying uncontrollably and thanking the jury for their verdict. Ms. Davis, the baby's mother who also had witnessed the jury's verdict, simultaneously jumped to her feet. But Ms. Davis stood with her 38 handgun that she had carefully slipped into the courtroom and exclaimed, "No, no, not guilty! But guilty!"

Ms. Davis with her hysterical announcement steadied her two arms and ten fingers wrapped around her pearl handled handgun and shot Mr. Edgar Fielding. As Fielding's body fell to the floor, the court's bailiff, Isaac Martin, quickly rushed to his side finding a shallow heartbeat. Seconds seemed like hours as the emergency management service desperately arrived to keep Fielding alive and the emergency ride to the hospital seemed to Fielding like one of his carefully orchestrated funeral wakes.

The District Attorney, Edward Johnson, the county sheriff, Randall Ashe, and the county coroner, Robert Crest Field gathered at the hospital's room door as if they were in an Arizona desert of 1878, speaking with an American Indian about signing a much sought land treaty. As they spoke, Fielding intently, with his big deer-type ears, sensed that Mr. Johnson, the District Attorney, was the real leader.

Johnson said, "We must bring a safe environment to our small Westbury community and the only way is to get old Fielding out, finally out of the way." Hearing this rather startling assertion, Fielding thought they were gonna kill him but soon discovered that there was a Massachusetts' program that allowed authorities who felt real threats to their community's citizens could quietly transport the person from the community to assume a different identity. After much discussion, a death certificate would be created for one, Edgar Fielding, which included a grand Westbury funeral with a quiet and hasty burial at Westbury Heights cemetery. Fielding could be forever protected from all others who sought revenge.

As the three most powerful men of Westbury stood around Fielding's bedside, Fielding heard Sheriff Ashe as he said, "If he lives in our community, he will always be endangered and would be like a forever suspect. We must all commit to our plan for it is in the best interest of our Westbury's community."

Fielding surmised that their agreement was much like his friend, Attorney Tom's adoption plan. The edges of Fielding's mouth slowly began to quietly and sharply curl to his eyelids. Smiling, Fielding knew that he would have his own death scheme but this time created by the three most powerful citizens of Westbury. As he became folded like an accordion in his hospital bed, he looked casually into the misty veil of life and looked upon the three men as once again Gershwin's rhapsody began to slowly play and large and pronounced puddles of tears came to his water-soaked brown eyes and very rosy cheeks. Once again, the curved edges of his mouth entertained his long, straight nose and his spectacles became misty.

Fielding began moving away from his deceitful past into a new future while also thinking that all it required was one bullet from a stranger's 38 handgun and not his own. He remembered the day he had been in his dusty funeral parlor's office asking God for a miracle. He thought of Nancy and Tom and how they could happily live the rest of their lives on the illegal monies and how each of them, Fielding, Nancy, and Tom would boldly survive their deceitful journey.

7

Tom Lawson Esquire could now relax because Edgar Fielding's gravesite lay in Westbury Heights Cemetery with its large tombstone. He and Nancy watched as Fielding funeral home's hearse rolled quietly to his grave site and a large wooden coffin was quickly covered by a layer of dirt storing it for eternity. Relief was indescribable for Nancy and Tom, it was as if an unpredictable storm had finally moved on its course and a peacefulness had returned to Elm Street. Now, Tom could share the rest of his life with his beloved, Nancy and with the profits from the adoptions. Day by marvelous day passed, followed by year after marvelous year as Tom and Allie divorced and Tom and Nancy became husband and wife. Nancy continued to deliver babies at Amherst Hospital. Tom retired and continued having his daily Negronis while continuing to manicure their lawn to perfection.

Allie, having regretted ever marrying Tom, decided to move and return north to Nova Scotia for the Canadian region was where her best childhood memories had been created. As she carefully packed to leave 12 years of sitting and listening to Tom, old photo albums and long since discarded clothing appeared from the Lawsons' dusty closets while her former residence of 116 Elm Street began to become a ghostly place. Soon Allie's 1970 Ford Taurus drove away to her new life. Allie begin to think as she drove away:

"Good bye, Tom,
You left my life so long ago
Remember when we were young
Your law shingle sparkled
In the summer sun
Oh, what joy was upon that wood;

Now, your ol' shingle
Fades
Showing
Nothing but dishonesty,
Deceit and lies."

As Allie carefully drove away from Westbury's Elm Street, Tom and Nancy prospered in their new world created from their illegality and joyfully, eight months into their marriage, the happy couple had a son named Arthur, a happy surprise for Tom because he never knew that Nancy was pregnant during the trial. As the years passed, Arthur excelled, attending the same law school as his father and becoming a better lawyer than his father. Time took its toll on Tom. Years of alcohol abuse required a major liver operation and as he lay in Amherst Hospital. Tom thought of the wrongs of his life especially the precious babies whose parents he had deceived. Once again, baby after baby appeared in his mind and with each baby the dread of knowing he was wrong weighted on his conscience. Fearing death, his doctor at Amherst Memorial Hospital, Dr. Gracie Horn attended to his severe medical needs. One day, as she came into the room, gorgeous and friendly, Tom heard one curious statement Dr. Horn made. She said that she had been adopted and that her mother was also a doctor. Dr. Horn's conscience always spoke to her predicament in poem and she shared it with Tom:

"I was a child, born on October 7, 1959
Created by some unknowns
As I grew, I thought
Who am I?

As I went to sleep I would say,
Someday, I may
Meet and find
The truth
Hidden from me

But until then
I doctor the sick
For all life has meaning
Including my own."

As Tom lay, he wondered whether this doctor had been one of the children from their adoption plot. The liver operation went well and his son Arthur was taken with Dr. Horn's beauty leading to romance and eventually a marriage where Dr. Grace Horn became Dr. Grace Horn-

Lawson. Tom regretted his life and wondered whether he would be alive to see his grandchildren.

"A drop of drink was my first intention;
Yet, one drop became two
I didn't know that
The whisky bottle held a river;

A river of joy
As it ran thorough
My body and
Changed my life eternally."

Life became somewhat better for Tom, but curiously, he could not forget his daughter-in-law's statement. This began an investigation and one night while searching through his old oak desk and legal records, through all of the babies that were adopted, Tom found as he sat in his home's office's desk, a note. While gripping his two arms and ten fingers around the old frayed note, he found an original birth certificate of a baby girl and born on the same day as Dr. Horn. This note led Tom to believe that maybe Dr. Gracie Horn-Lawson was really his daughter, for it said,

"Tom, be careful with this one, for this daughter is mine. Find a good home. Nancy."

Fearing death, Tom decided that it was best to tell Nancy concerning their 'daughter-in-law', Gracie. As he spoke, large tears began coming from Tom as Nancy asked, "Why are you so sad?"

"Because Dr. Horn is my daughter and if I only had known, I wouldn't have let Arthur marry her."

As Nancy stumbled, she said, "Yes, I hear you, but, well, I can't believe Dr. Horn is really my Heather. I led Fielding to believe she was his daughter. I never told Fielding that I had become pregnant with your child." Tom's trust was shattered. He started doubting his life and the people in his life as he took a careful look at his son, Arthur. Tom always suspected that Arthur didn't have quite his facial features, so he nervously dialed the telephone to Allie.

"Allie, forgive me, but I must know…Is Arthur my son?"

Quietness came to the telephone call, and after several minutes, Allie holding the telephone with her two arms and ten fingers gradually said, "Fielding and I had an affair, and yes, Arthur is Fielding's, not yours. But you know a judge once said, 'If you feed a child long enough, he would be yours.' Good bye."

With this finding that his son Arthur was not his but Fielding's, Tom began to drink more and more, eventually leading to another hospitalization.

As he lay in another hospital bed at Amherst Hospital with death's shadow walking through the hospital's corridors, Dr. Horn-Lawson found that Tom's vital signs were drifting to a fatal end. As Tom lay, he began to speak:

"This is my end,
Yet, shall it be a beginning
Deceit, however, has no future
It is a lonely bird

One that flies not south
As the cold wind blows.
Autumn turns to Winter and
This bird begins to regret
Winter's choice
Other birds
Dance, happy and gay
In the southern air
Awaiting the Spring.

This bird holds on until others find out
And deceit
Becomes a death ring
Oh, how I see my deceitfulness
Now, but it's too late
I shall not go south
But wait on the final
Snow of Winter."

As he felt death near, Tom Lawson Esquire turned to the right side of his hospital bed and said, "My son Arthur, be blessed." He quickly turned to the left side of his hospital bed where Dr. Horn-Lawson stood and said, "My daughter, Gracie, your real name is Heather. Be blessed." Tom Lawson Esquire quietly passed into eternity.

8

Dejected, Nancy felt hollow and anxious as she prepared for Tom's funeral. She next thought that she will let the minister say only a few words, a simple graveside service at Westbury Heights Cemetery; Tom wouldn't have wanted anything more.

Fielding funeral home's hearse slowly passed Amherst Hospital and Magnolia Community Park, entering the huge wrought-iron gates of Westbury Heights Cemetery with Tom's remains. He was buried leaving a space for Nancy and only steps from Fielding's empty grave. After the funeral, Nancy slowly walked into their 114 Elm Street home and past the lawn that showed a lack of perfection and curiously decided to search Tom's desk.

Tom seemed to organize everything, but the room smelled extremely dusty and in his large oak desk, in a center drawer, appeared three items, one letter to Nancy, his Last Will and Testament, and a 38 handgun. She placed all three on Tom's large oak desk within the dusty desk's top and slowly opened the letter she nervously held with her two arms and ten fingers as her large broad nose was well-centered upon the words and between her very rosy cheeks. She cried.

Tom had written in the letter:

"We must pay for all our sins. We either pay doing life or in the afterlife. My soul is weary and I know the wrongs I have done. I know the wrongs we all did: you, me, and Fielding. All will come to the light of life and you should pray and do your best to make amends before it's too late. Death shall come like a strong stallion horse ready for its eternal journey and that is why I now use my two arms and ten fingers to write this letter. I summon your universal ethical essence to find a way to make peace and relieve your conscience from our deceitful ways. I also write my Last Will and Testament and leave all my worldly goods to Allie, for she was the one who always told me the truth and she had my trust and I abused her confidence in me while destroying our relationship."

As Nancy opened the Last Will and Testament with her aged two arms and ten fingers, she saw that Tom had indeed left everything to Allie.

"I, Tom Lawson, being of sound mind and body, do hereby leave all my worldly goods to my former wife, Allie Lawson. Please bury me quietly, but it is my wish to lay beside my present wife. Dr. Nancy Kilburn Fielding Lawson."

Feeling the weight of her deceit, she thought:

I have seen life come forth
With cries and wails

All now I can think
Is death.

A dark light after the bright
Lights of life was my soul.
I can only blame
One that is me

As now my journey
Ends.
Goodbye to Sydney, Royce, Jefferson
And all the precious babies
I've known;

Good bye to the old oak tree
Good bye, to life
Where I had hoped to be
Virtuous and free.

I chose a pathway of deceit,
The money I did make.
I now cannot help myself

I pull this trigger
And the pall shall cover me
To have judgment now
Rather than to patiently wait.

Calmly, Nancy raised Tom's 38 pearl-handled handgun from the desk and, with her two arms and ten fingers, fired a bullet that finally solved her entire situation. The doctor's body was placed between her two husbands, Edgar Fielding and Tom Lawson Esquire, at Westbury Heights Cemetery as the entire communities of Milton and Westbury came out to stand around her ornate wooden coffin; look upon the professional embalming and honor a much beloved obstetrician and friend.

9

As the year 1989 became a wintry season, a cool breezy winter wind blew gently through the snow covered trees of Westbury, Massachusetts. The 1970 Ford Taurus drove cautiously and slowly through the wrought-iron gates of Westbury Heights Cemetery passing Amherst Hospital and one large oak tree at Magnolia Community Park. The car came slowly to a definitive stop as a lone figure exited the vehicle and moved quietly through the many large tombstones. The person quietly walked as the snow crushed underneath her small weathered shoes protecting her small red toes and aged legs. As she arrived at three gravestones that were blanketed somewhat by the snowfall, the petite lady silently whispered to herself:

"As I return to look
Upon history,
I walk along these
Stones of life;
Cold white stones,
All covered
In snowflakes
Falling from the chilly Westbury sky,

Many stones
Have no name
Yet, proof once there was
Indeed life

Let
Me see the three
I seek now;
God, unfold that to me."

Three specific snow-covered grave sites that had large tombstones awaited this curious visitor as the frostiness of the air touched her delicate skin. Her once-nimble fingers became cold and ached for relief with the white flowered gloves in her blue overcoat's pocket. Carefully and methodically, the visitor walked to the first tombstone, one of Mr. Edgar Fielding whose epitaph read:

"Here sleeps one who with his two arms and ten fingers assisted others who now lay at eternal rest. His precious spirit took flight after a jury found him innocent when his innocence as an inalienable right was so presumed in life."

This lone visitor then stepped to the second tombstone with an epitaph that read:

"Dr. Nancy Kilburn Fielding-Lawson: Here sleeps a beloved doctor and mother who was helped by her two arms and ten fingers to assist precious children coming into this world. Her spirit helped nurture many a baby so as to introduce them to the wonders of life."

The third gravesite, dark and gray, announced the gravesite of Mr. Thomas Lawson Esquire. It was at this gravesite, the visitor started to cry. Through her tears, she began to read the epitaph on the large tombstone:

"Here sleeps a lawyer who with his two arms and ten fingers used his legal skills to assist others to live in this interesting world. He insisted on Perfection, Perfection, Perfection and gave many a new life by the stroke of a pen."

The visitor saw that her tears had disturbed the snow upon this particular tombstone, and with her two arms and ten fingers, she slowly took from her long winter coat, a small handkerchief.

Seconds seemed like days as she wiped the drops of her tears that lay on the tombstone. Her silence was broken by another figure who had been in the passenger seat of the 1970 Ford Taurus. As he walked up to the lonely visitor bowing over the third tombstone, he reached out to hold her hand and stop her from dusting further snow from the tombstone with his two arms and ten fingers. She in turn began to move her two arms and ten fingers and laced her small hands within his large hands which still smelled of formaldehyde and death. The passenger began to slowly speak, "We can only stay a short while. I find myself old and looking upon my former life and as I turn and see your beautiful eyes, I continue to see my future, not our past. Let us continue to move forward into our life, keeping our promises now and away from the despair of the past before we also sleep."

As the snow continued to gently fall from Westbury's gray sky, two figures in the snowy late-afternoon winter's day stood there, standing over three gravesites.

He said, "Deceit can be beautiful. Just depends on who benefits. Allie, we must go."

And she said, "Yes, Fielding, we must go. Yes, we must go."

Epilogue

Whose woods these are, I think I know,
His house is in the village though;
He will not see me stopping here
To watch his woods, fill up with snow.
My little horse must think it queer
To stop without a farmhouse near
Between the woods and frozen lake
The darkest evening of the year.

He gives his harness bells a shake
To ask if there is some mistake.
The only other sound's the sweep
Of easy wind and downy flake.

The woods are lovely, dark and deep,
But I have promises to keep,
And miles to go before I sleep,
And miles to go before I sleep.

"Stopping by woods on a snowy evening," Robert Frost

One must dare to be happy. It takes a lot of time to be a genius. You have to sit around so much, doing nothing, really doing nothing. Everybody knows if you are too careful, you are so occupied in being careful that you are sure to stumble over something.

Gertrude Stein
February 3, 1874
– July 27, 1946